Dear Parent:

Psst . . . you're looking at the Super Secret Weapon of Reading. It's called comics.

STEP INTO READING® COMIC READERS are a perfect step in learning to read. They provide visual cues to the meaning of words and helpfully break out short pieces of dialogue into speech balloons.

Here are some terms commonly associated with comics:

- PANEL: A section of a comic with a box drawn around it.
- CAPTION: Narration that helps set the scene.
- SPEECH BALLOON: A bubble containing dialogue.
- GUTTER: The space between panels.

SPEECH BALLOON
PANEL
I'm happy!
The next day.
CAPTION
GUTTER

Tips for reading comics with your child:

- Have your child read the speech balloons while you read the captions.
- Ask your child: What is a character feeling? How can you tell?
- Have your child draw a comic showing what happens after the book is finished.

STEP INTO READING® COMIC READERS are designed to engage and to provide an empowering reading experience. They are also fun. The best-kept secret of comics is that they create lifelong readers. **And that will make you the real hero of the story!**

Jennifer L. Holm and Matthew Holm
Co-creators of the Babymouse and Squish series

Jurassic World Franchise © 2021 Universal City Studios LLC and Amblin Entertainment, Inc.
Series © 2021 DreamWorks Animation LLC.. All Rights Reserved.

Published in the United States by Random House Children's Books, a division of
Penguin Random House LLC, 1745 Broadway, New York, NY 10019, and in Canada by
Penguin Random House Canada Limited, Toronto. Step into Reading, Random House,
and the Random House colophon are registered trademarks of Penguin Random House LLC.

Visit us on the Web!
StepIntoReading.com
rhcbooks.com

Educators and librarians, for a variety of teaching tools, visit us at RHTeachersLibrarians.com

ISBN 978-0-593-18029-7 (trade) — ISBN 978-0-593-30431-0 (lib. bdg.) —
ISBN 978-0-593-30432-7 (ebook)

Printed in the United States of America   10 9 8 7 6 5 4

STEP 3 READING ON YOUR OWN

STEP INTO READING®

A COMIC READER

JURASSIC WORLD

CAMP CRETACEOUS

LOST IN THE WILD!

adapted by Steve Behling
illustrated by Patrick Spaziante

Random House New York

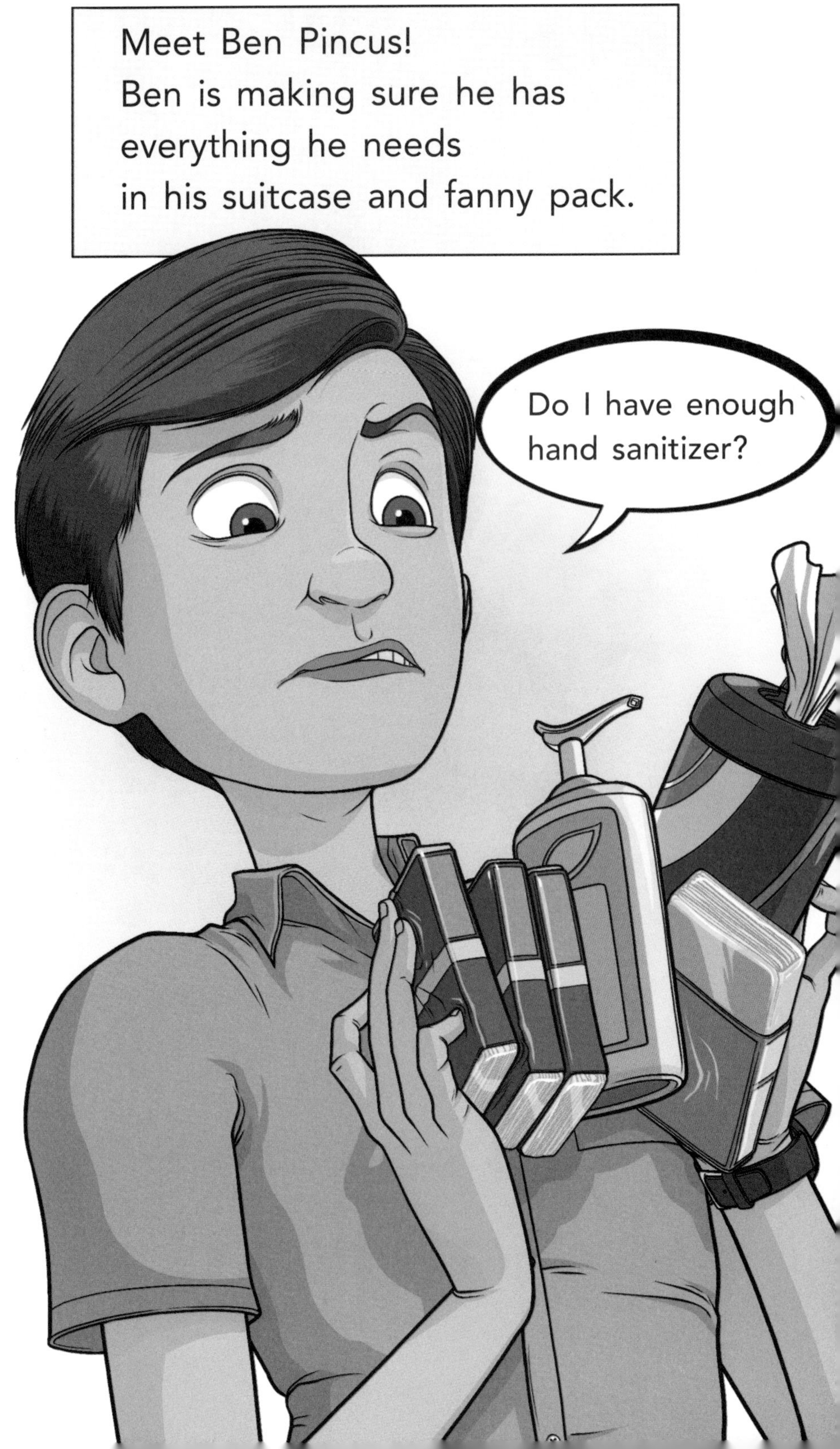
Meet Ben Pincus!
Ben is making sure he has
everything he needs
in his suitcase and fanny pack.
Do I have enough
hand sanitizer?

Ben is nervous.
He doesn't like
being away from home.

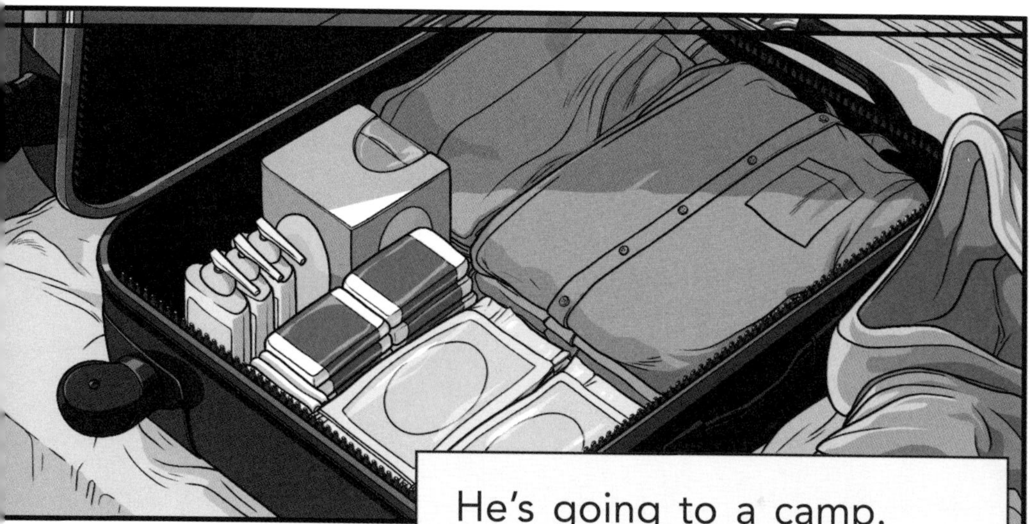

He's going to a camp.
But it's not just *any* camp.

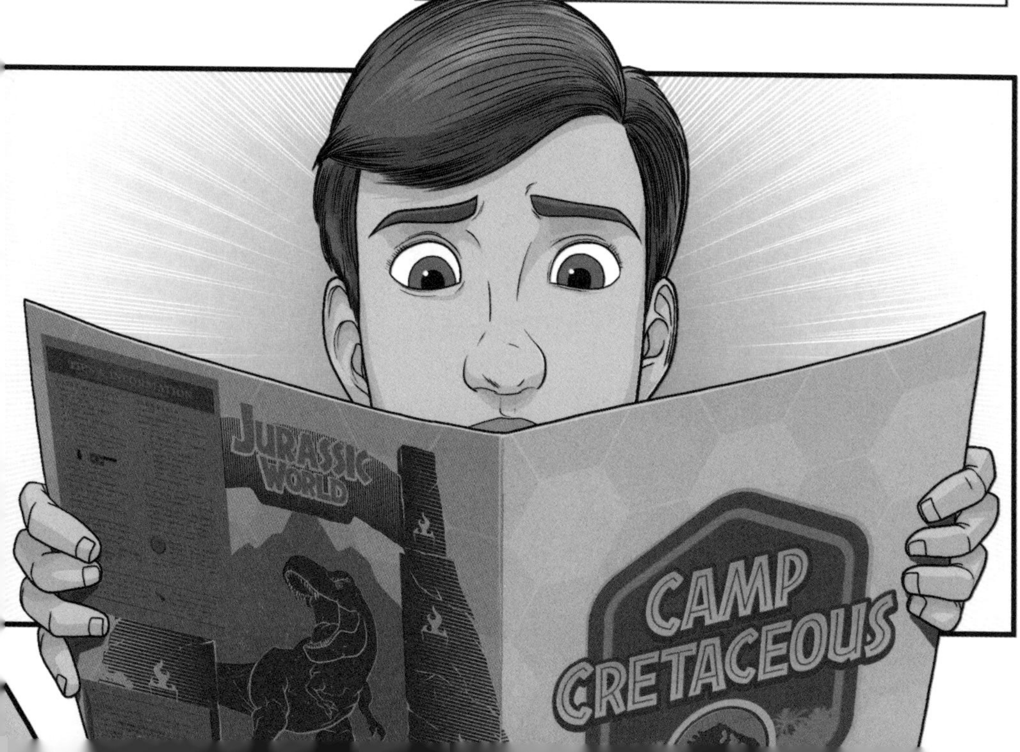
JURASSIC WORLD
CAMP CRETACEOUS

Ben is going to Camp Cretaceous!
It's at Jurassic World.
It may be the coolest camp ever!
He will be on an island . . .
with dinosaurs!

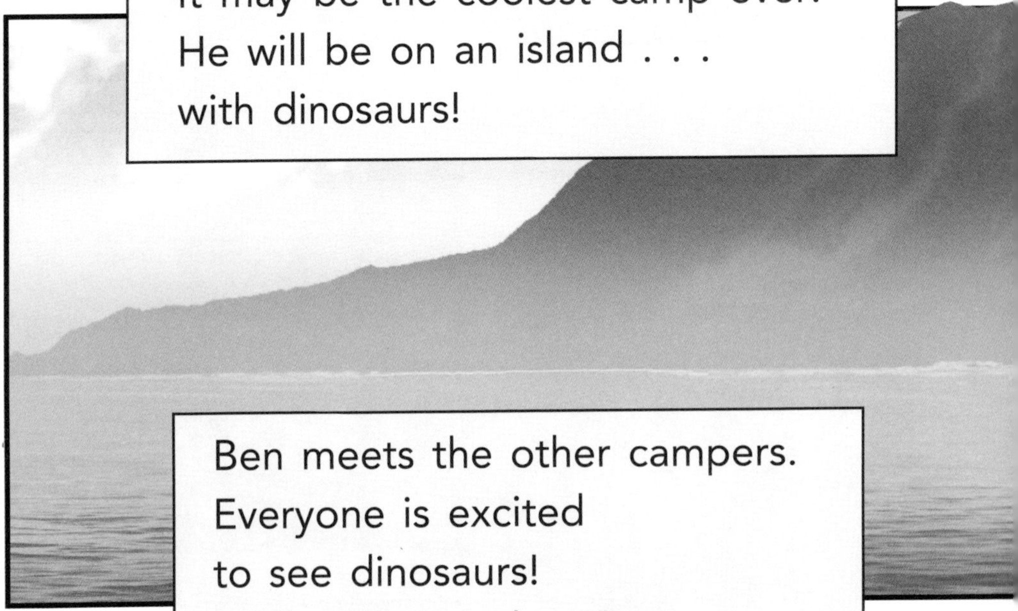

Ben meets the other campers.
Everyone is excited
to see dinosaurs!
Well, everyone but Ben.

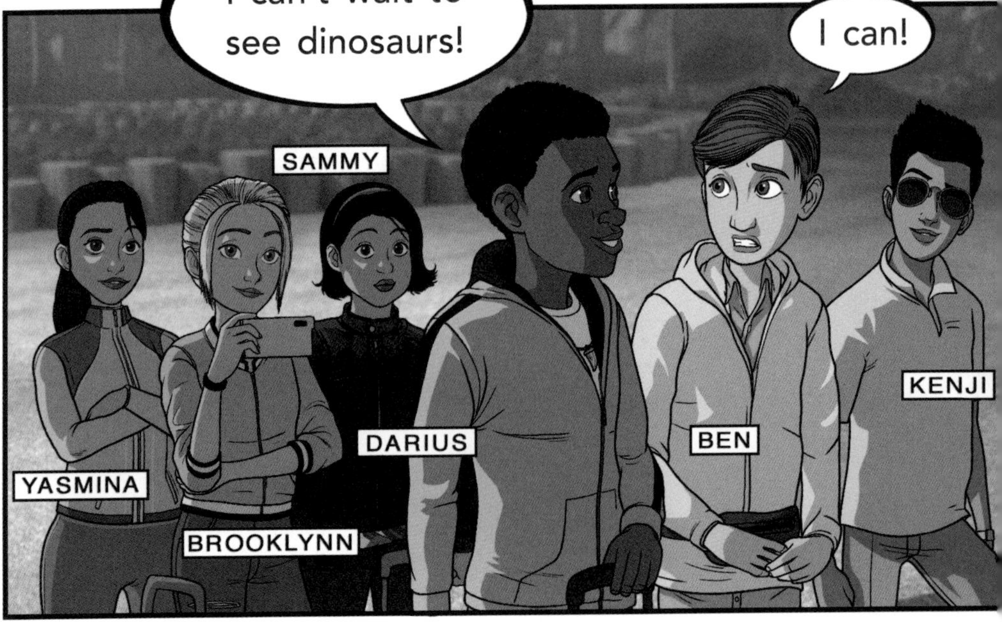
I can't wait to see dinosaurs!
I can!
SAMMY
KENJI
DARIUS
BEN
YASMINA
BROOKLYNN

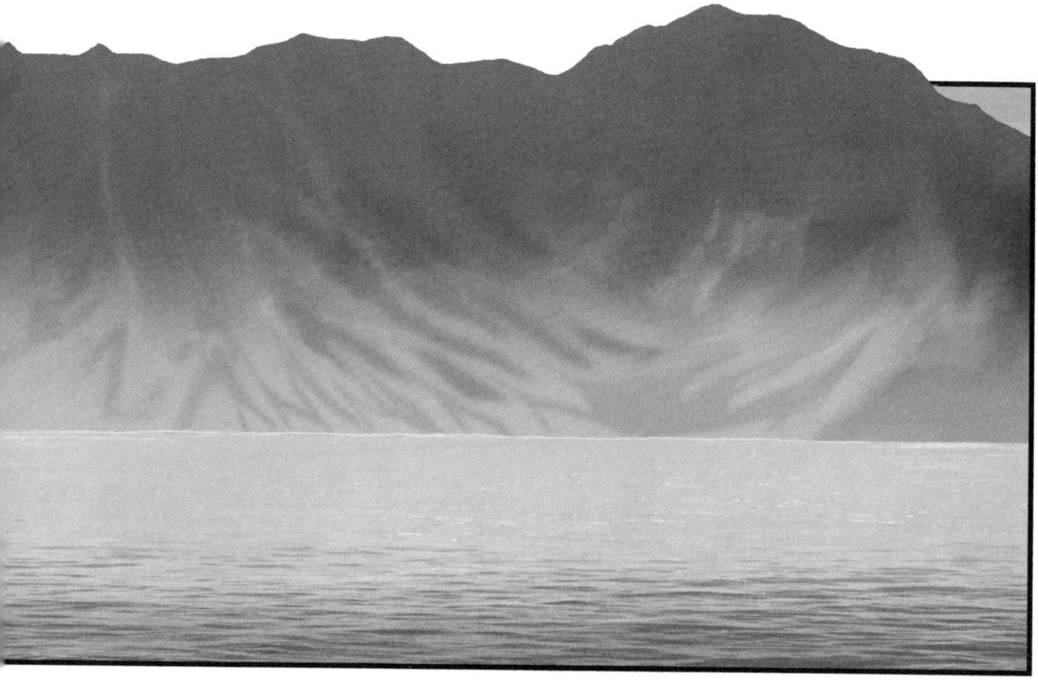

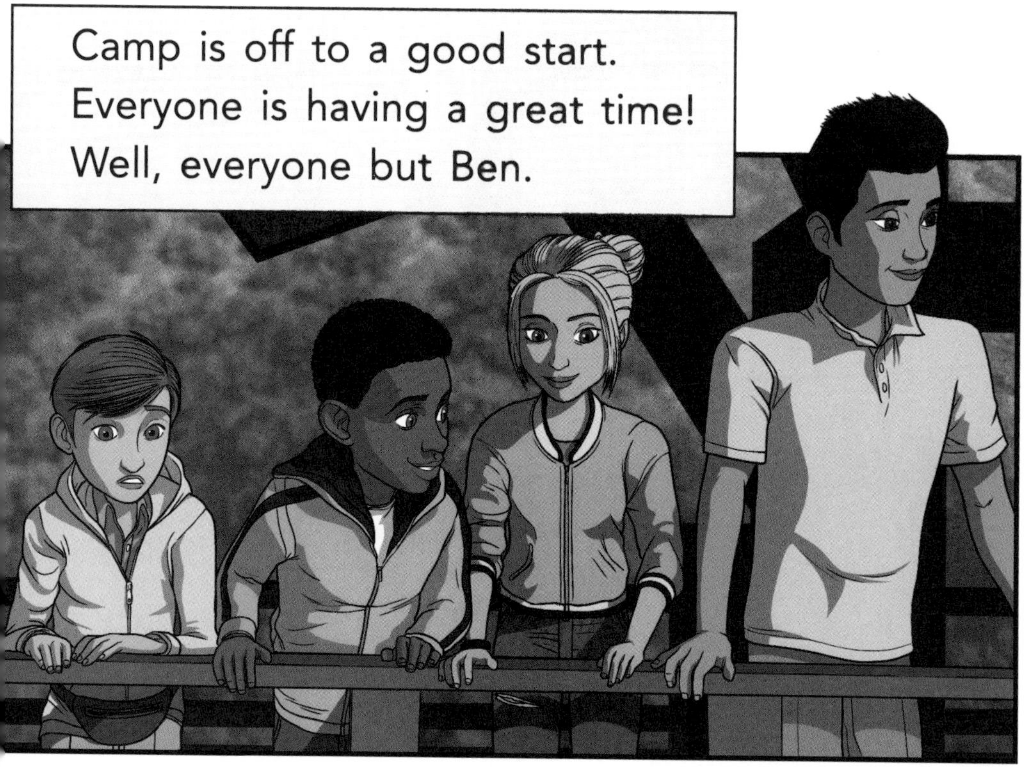
Camp is off to a good start.
Everyone is having a great time!
Well, everyone but Ben.

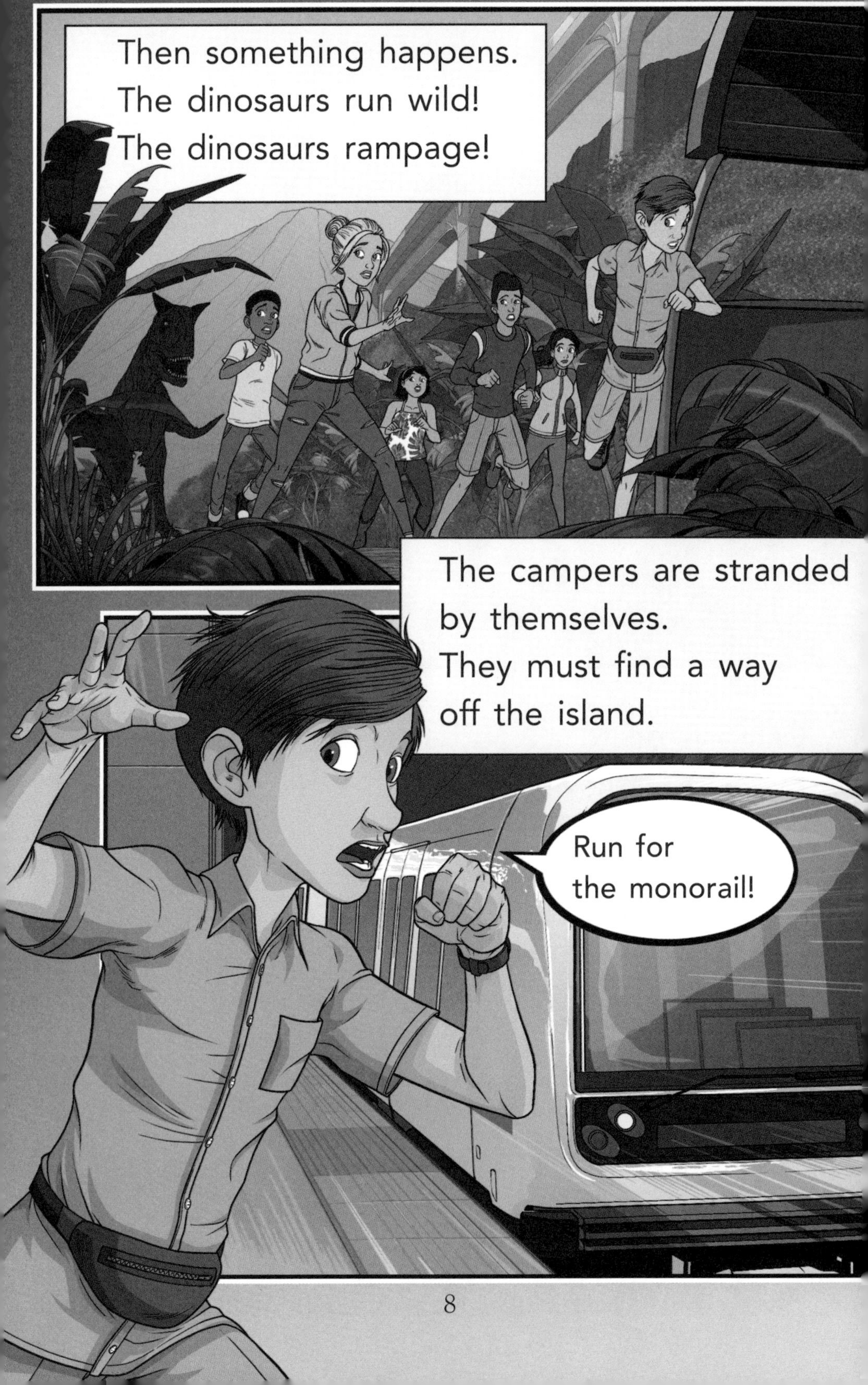
Then something happens.
The dinosaurs run wild!
The dinosaurs rampage!
The campers are stranded by themselves.
They must find a way off the island.
Run for the monorail!

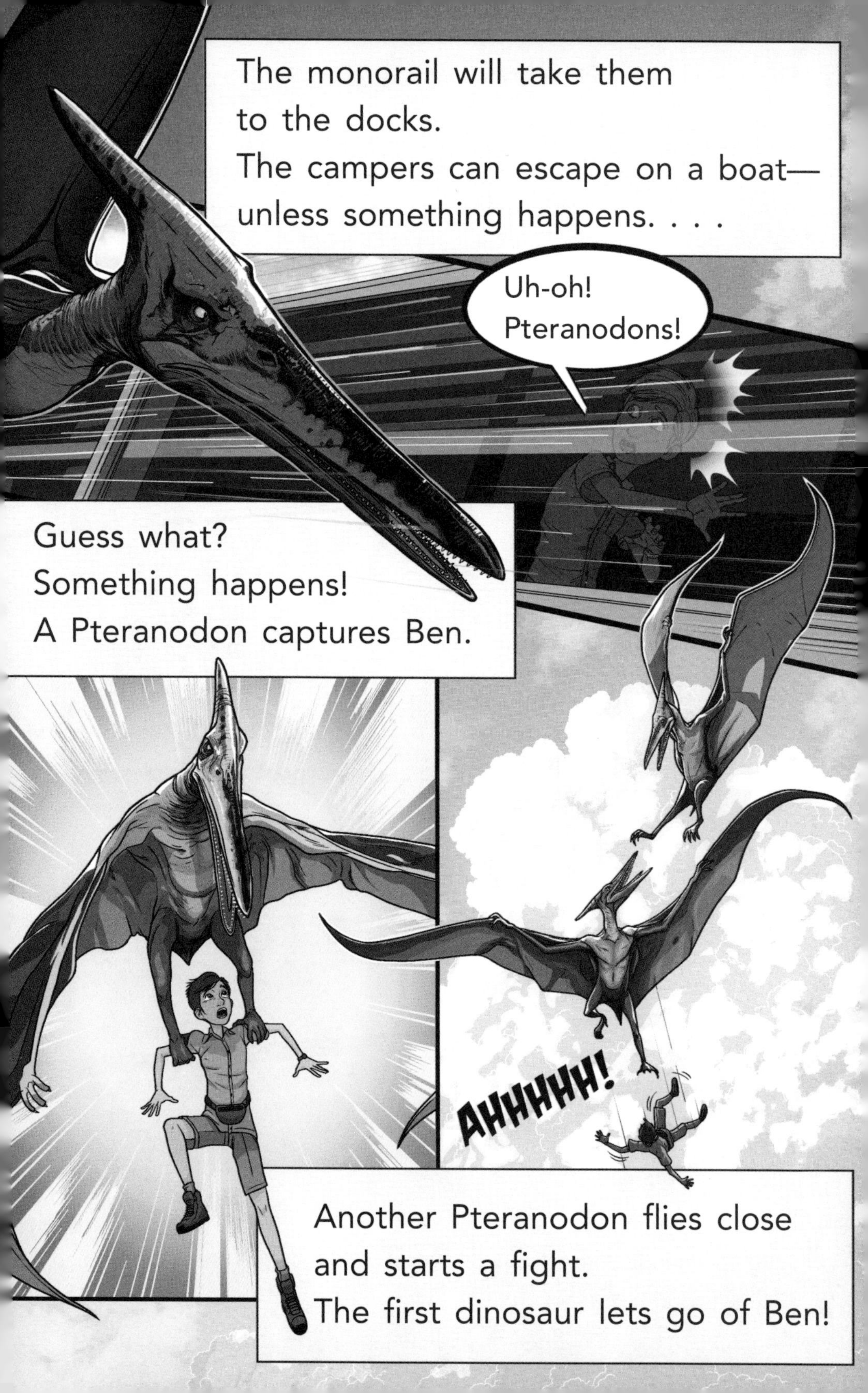
The monorail will take them to the docks. The campers can escape on a boat—unless something happens. . . .
Uh-oh! Pteranodons!
Guess what? Something happens! A Pteranodon captures Ben.
AHHHHH!
Another Pteranodon flies close and starts a fight. The first dinosaur lets go of Ben!

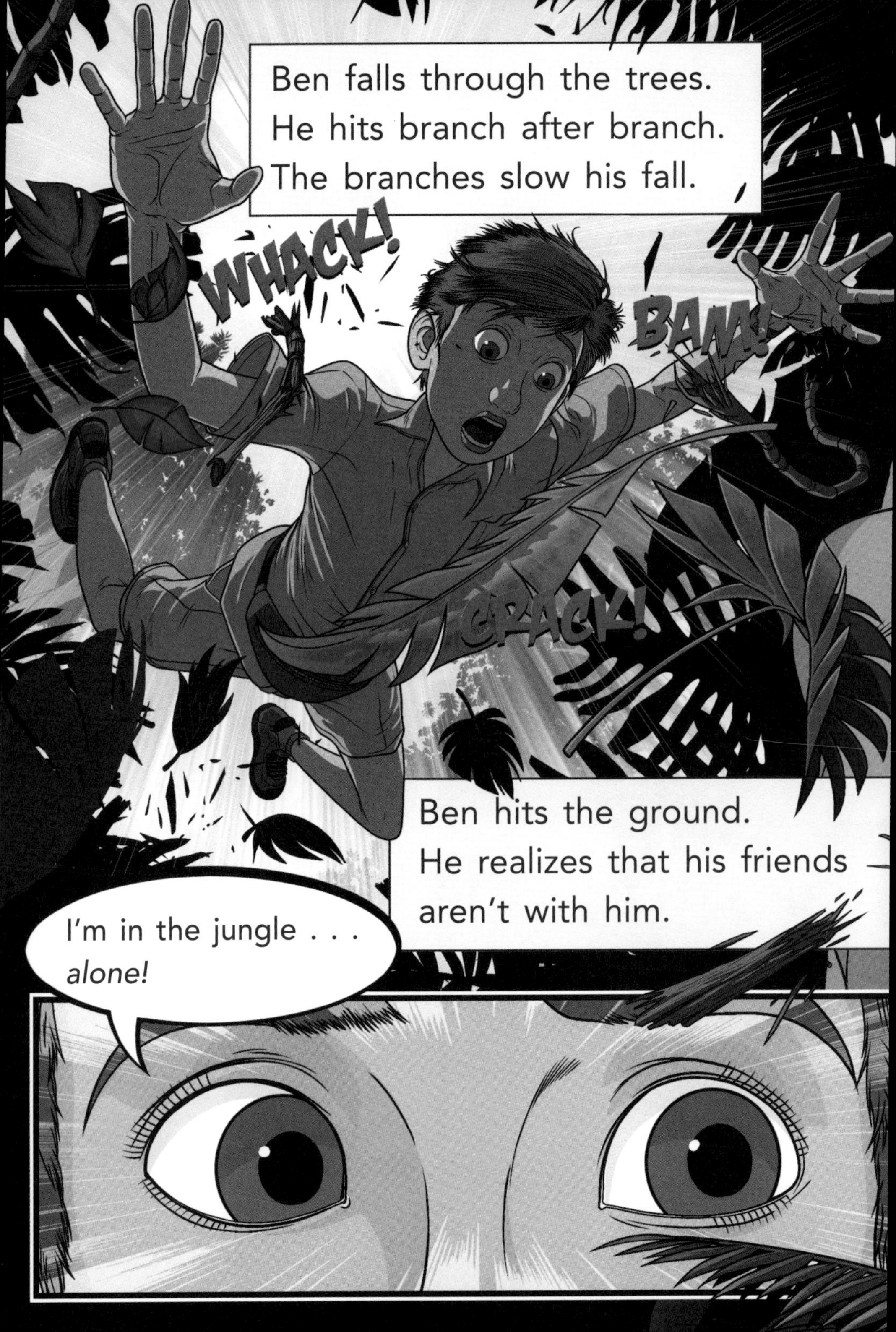
Ben falls through the trees.
He hits branch after branch.
The branches slow his fall.
WHACK!
BAM!
CRACK!
Ben hits the ground.
He realizes that his friends aren't with him.
I'm in the jungle . . . *alone!*

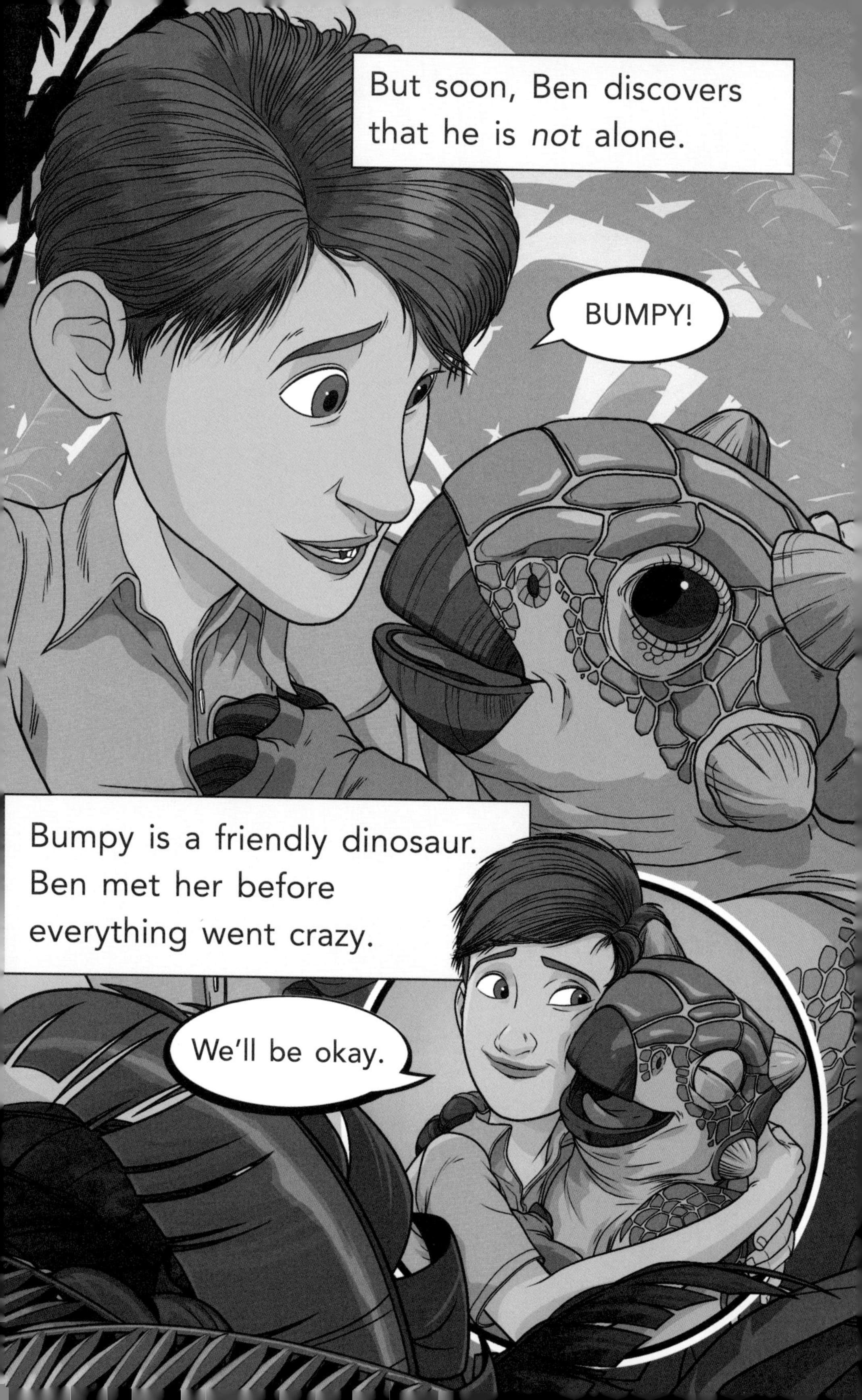
But soon, Ben discovers that he is *not* alone.
BUMPY!
Bumpy is a friendly dinosaur. Ben met her before everything went crazy.
We'll be okay.

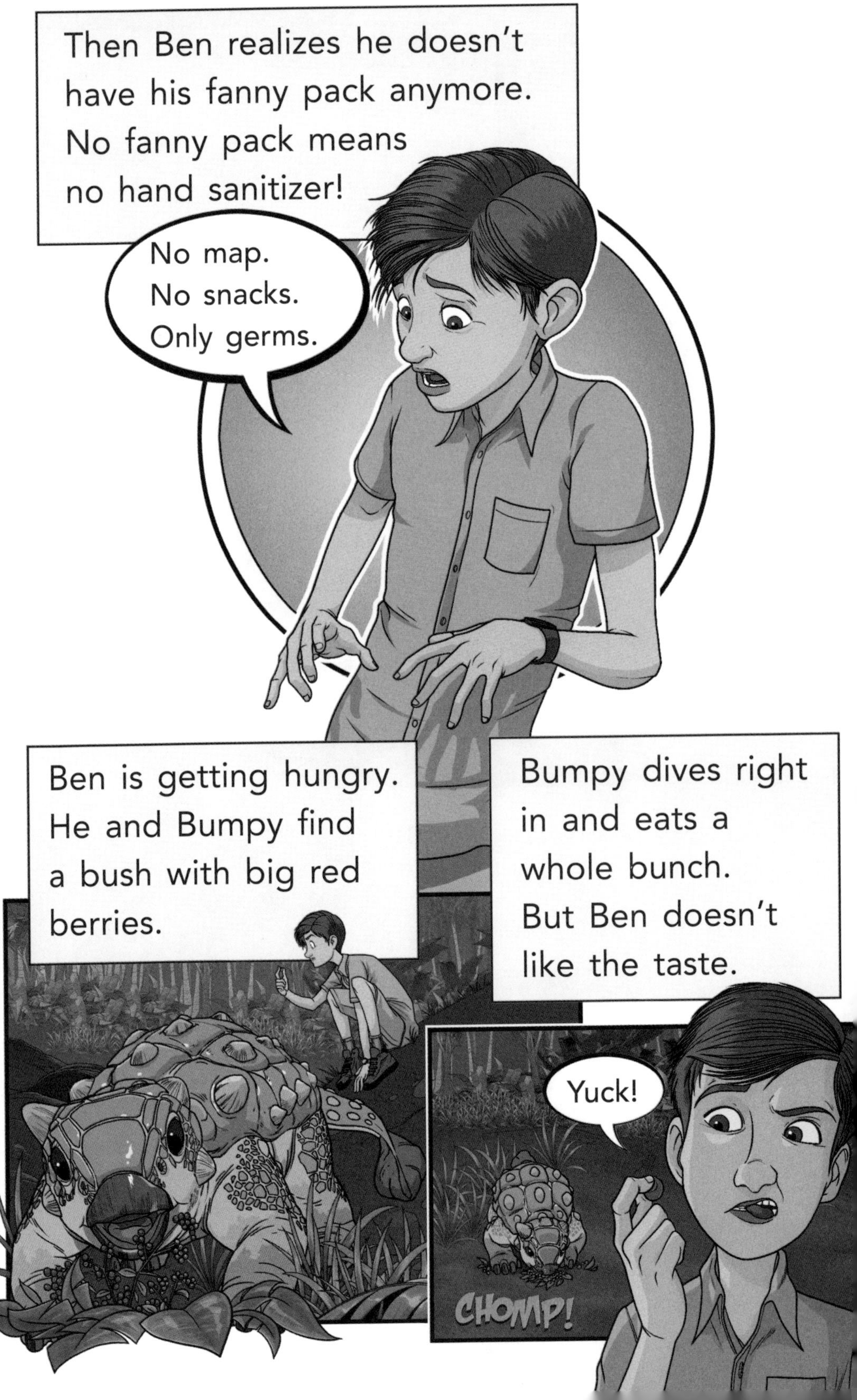
Then Ben realizes he doesn't have his fanny pack anymore. No fanny pack means no hand sanitizer!
No map. No snacks. Only germs.
Ben is getting hungry. He and Bumpy find a bush with big red berries.
Bumpy dives right in and eats a whole bunch. But Ben doesn't like the taste.
Yuck!
CHOMP!

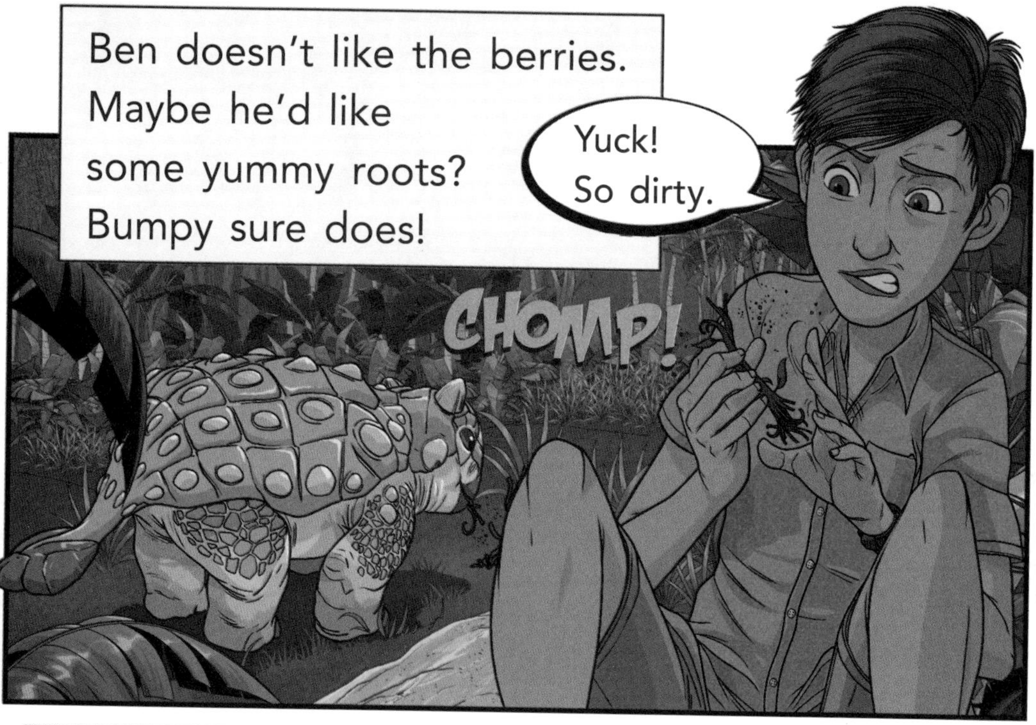
Ben doesn't like the berries. Maybe he'd like some yummy roots? Bumpy sure does!
Yuck! So dirty.
CHOMP!

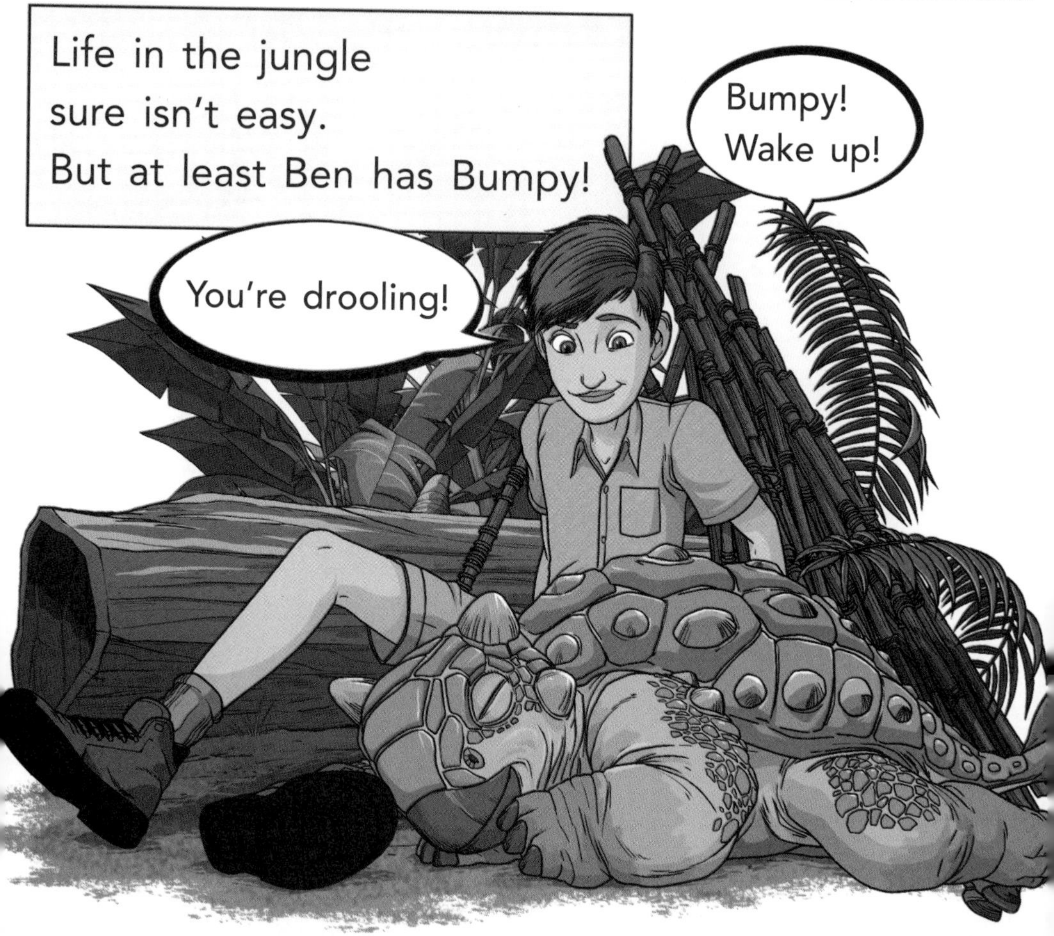
Life in the jungle sure isn't easy. But at least Ben has Bumpy!
Bumpy! Wake up!
You're drooling!

New plan. Go *this* way!
Ben tries to make the best of it. He and Bumpy decide to find a way off the island.

But Ben and Bumpy are in trouble. A Stegosaurus shows up and ruins their plan!
New plan! *Run!*

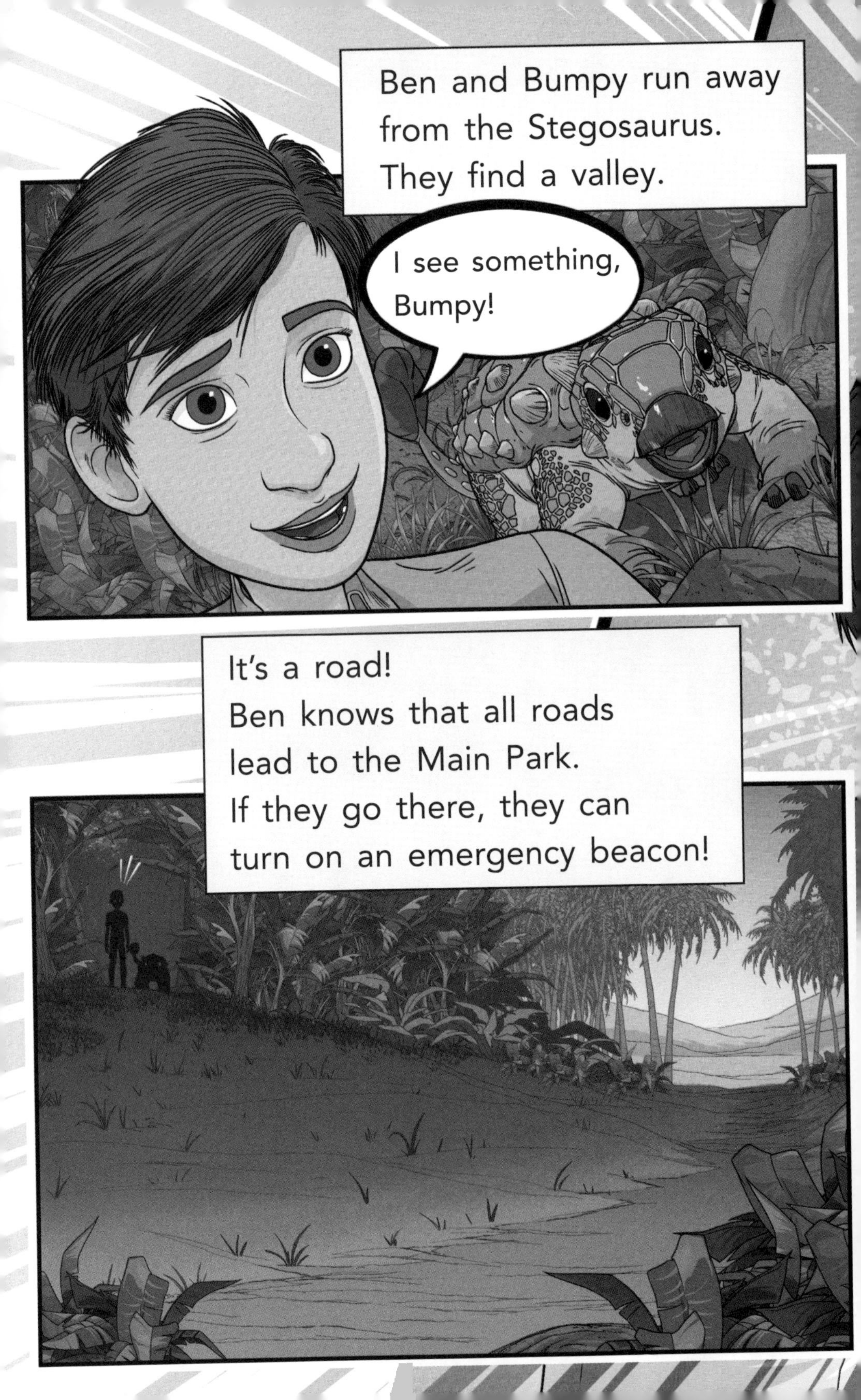
Ben and Bumpy run away from the Stegosaurus. They find a valley.
I see something, Bumpy!
It's a road! Ben knows that all roads lead to the Main Park. If they go there, they can turn on an emergency beacon!

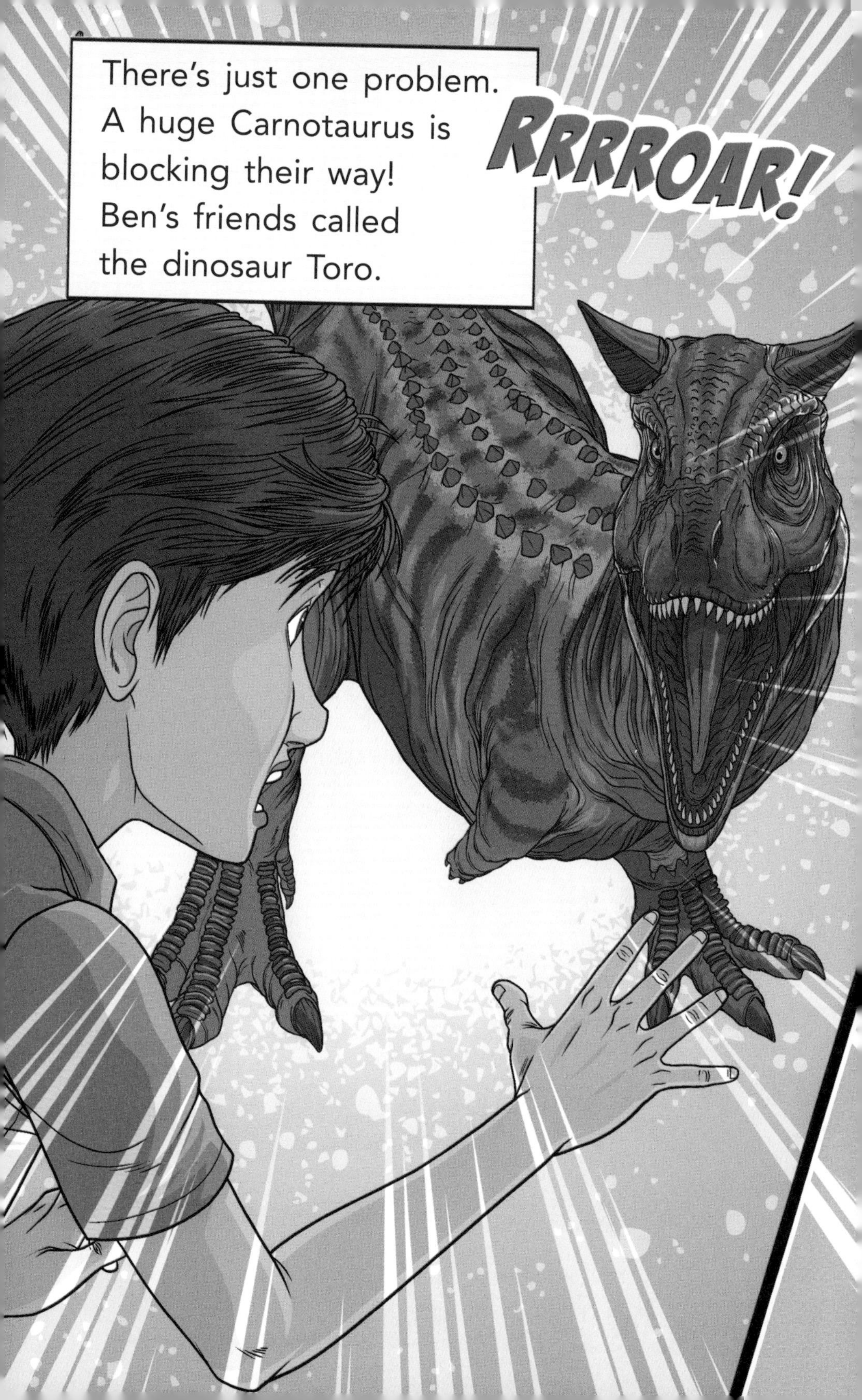
There's just one problem. A huge Carnotaurus is blocking their way! Ben's friends called the dinosaur Toro.
RRRROAR!

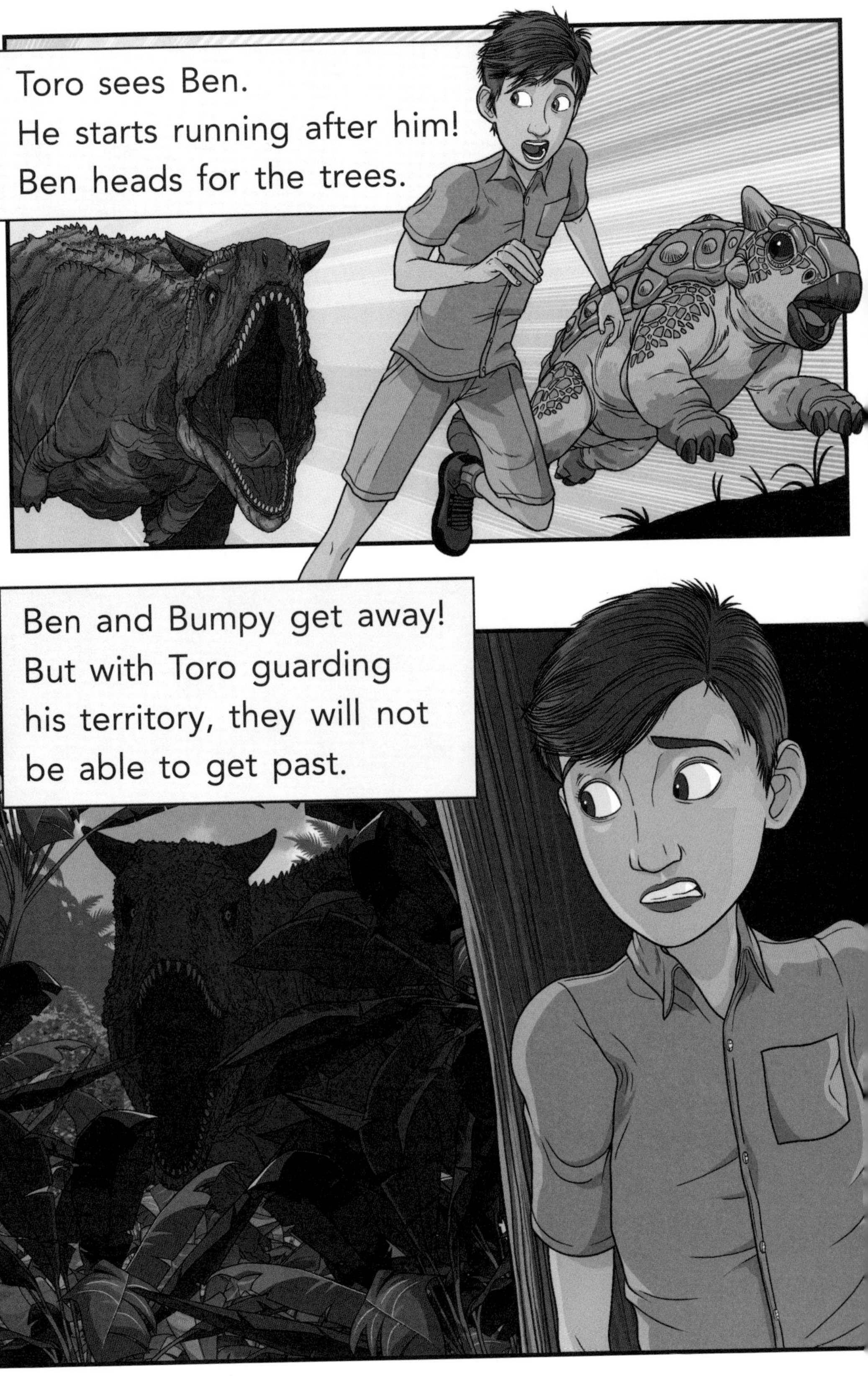
Toro sees Ben.
He starts running after him!
Ben heads for the trees.
Ben and Bumpy get away!
But with Toro guarding
his territory, they will not
be able to get past.

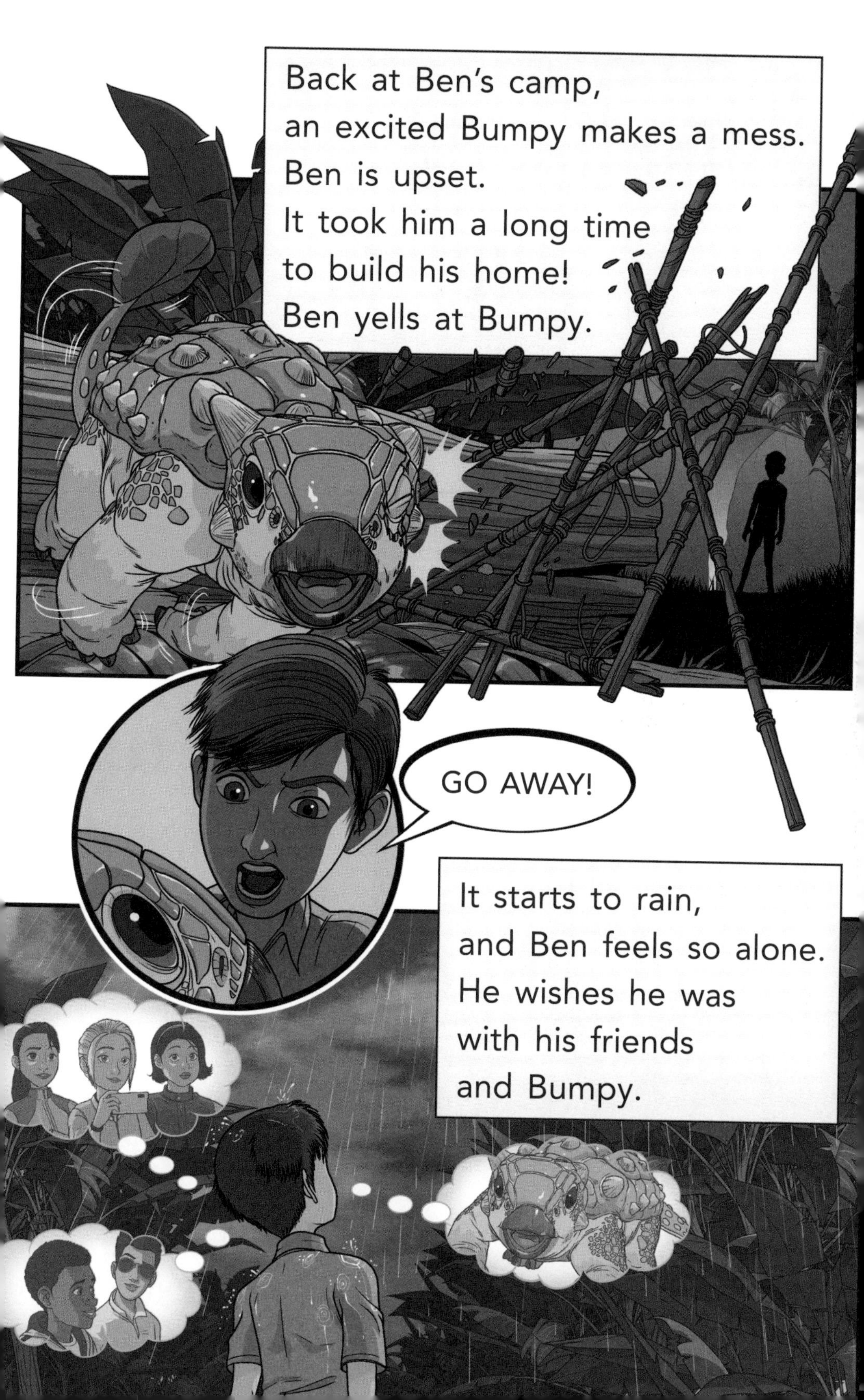
Back at Ben's camp,
an excited Bumpy makes a mess.
Ben is upset.
It took him a long time
to build his home!
Ben yells at Bumpy.
GO AWAY!
It starts to rain,
and Ben feels so alone.
He wishes he was
with his friends
and Bumpy.

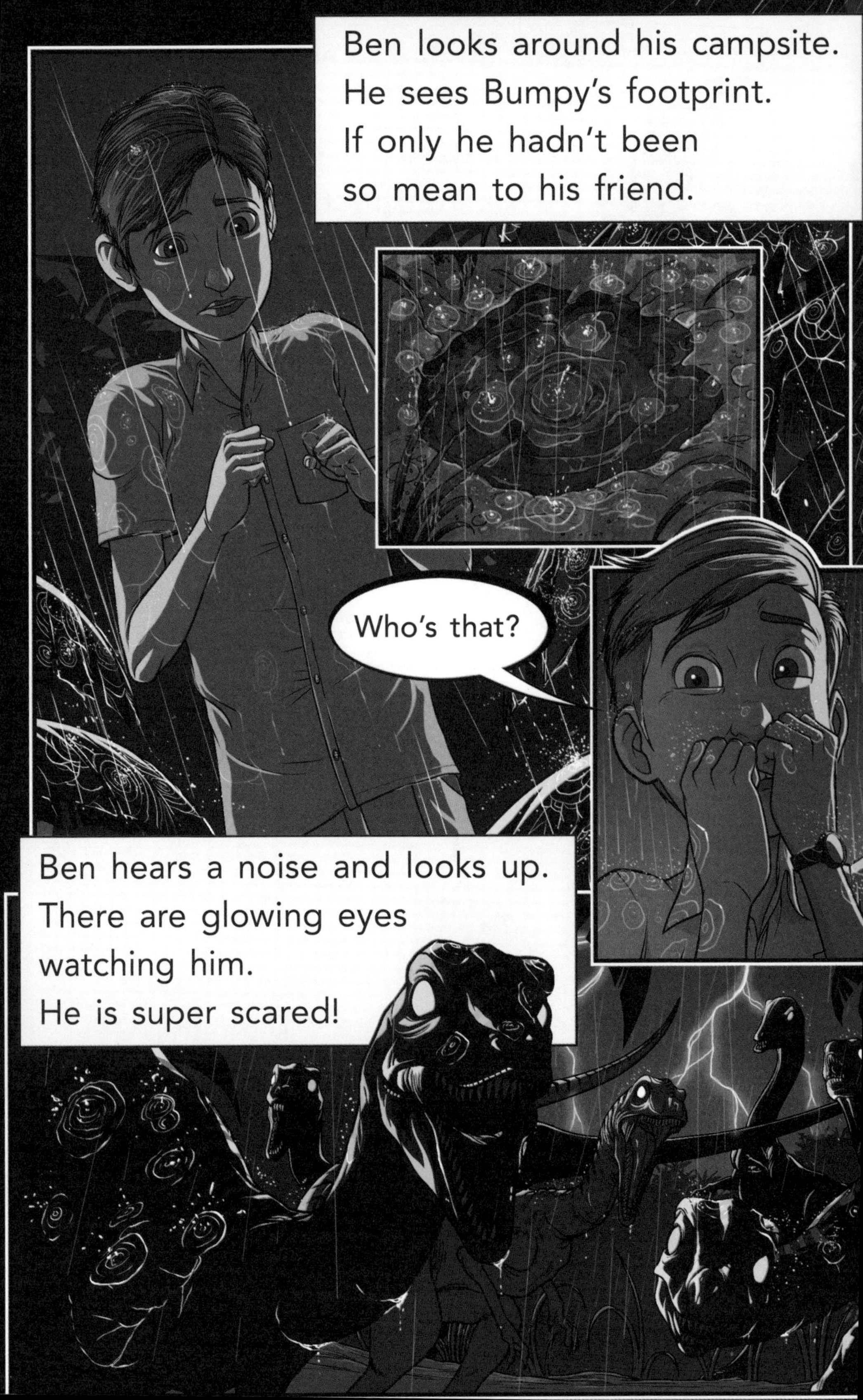

Ben looks around his campsite. He sees Bumpy's footprint. If only he hadn't been so mean to his friend.
Who's that?
Ben hears a noise and looks up. There are glowing eyes watching him. He is super scared!

A group of Compsognathuses chase Ben!
He runs as fast as he can, but the Compys follow.
Yikes!

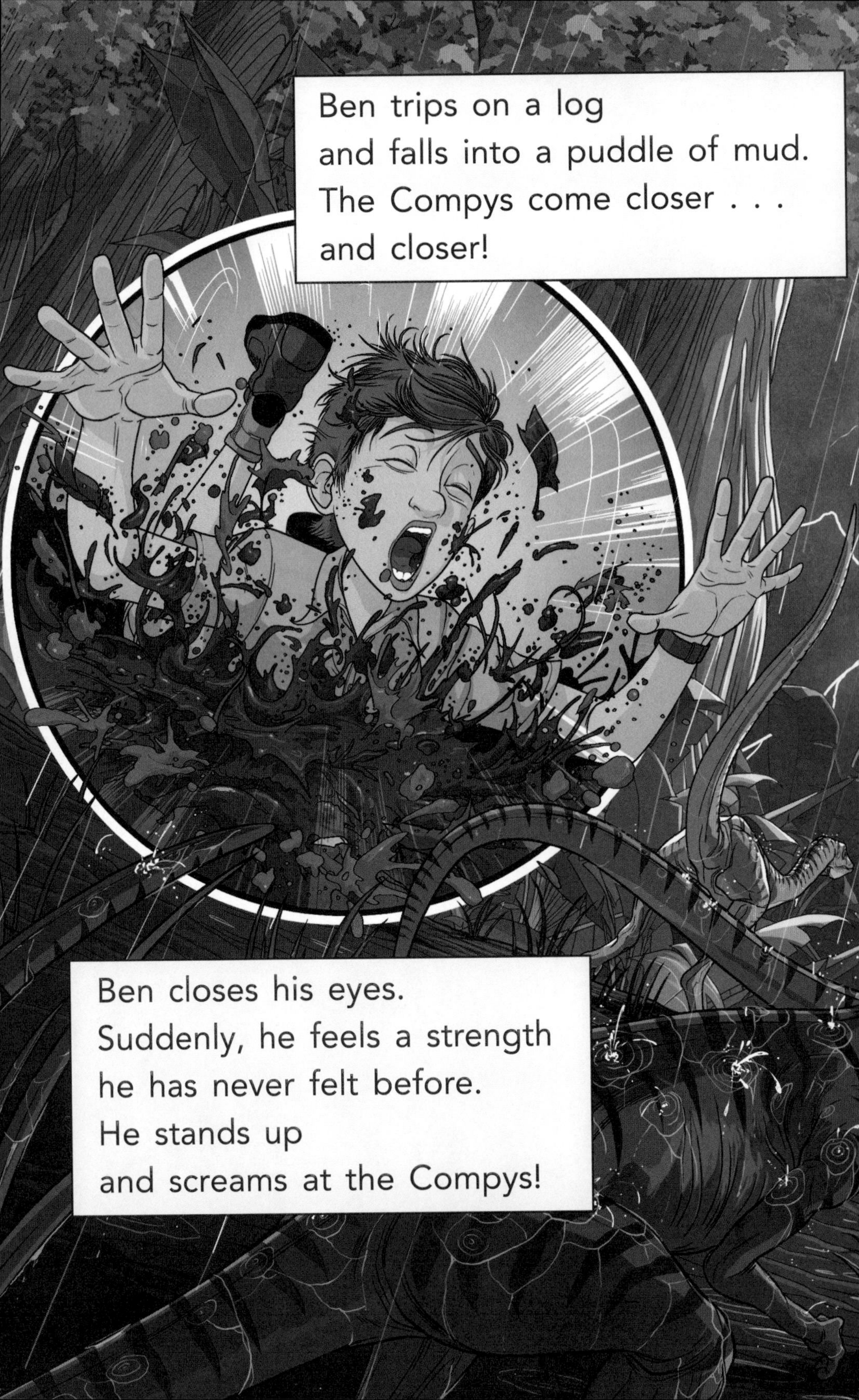
Ben trips on a log and falls into a puddle of mud. The Compys come closer . . . and closer!
Ben closes his eyes. Suddenly, he feels a strength he has never felt before. He stands up and screams at the Compys!

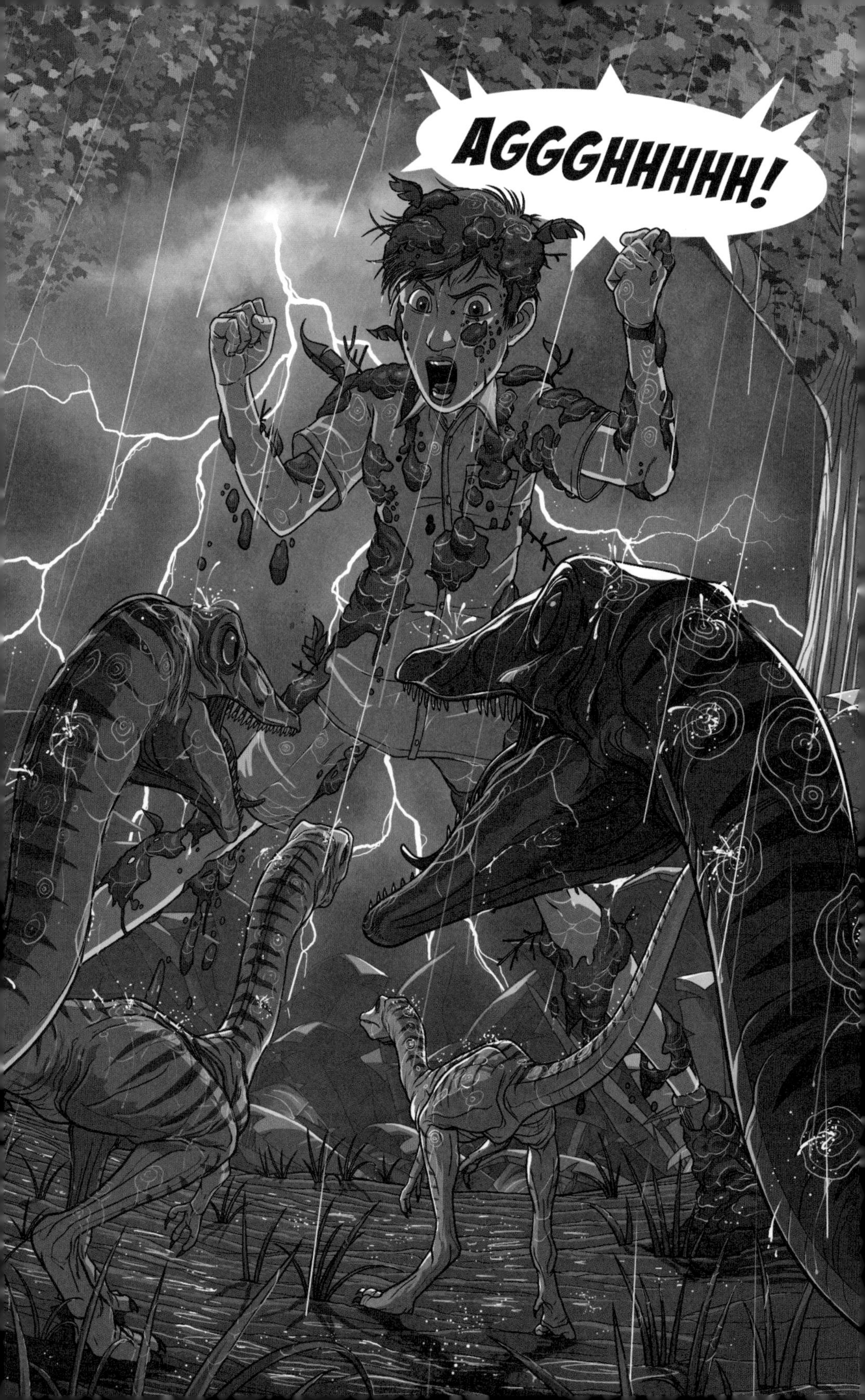
AGGGHHHHH!

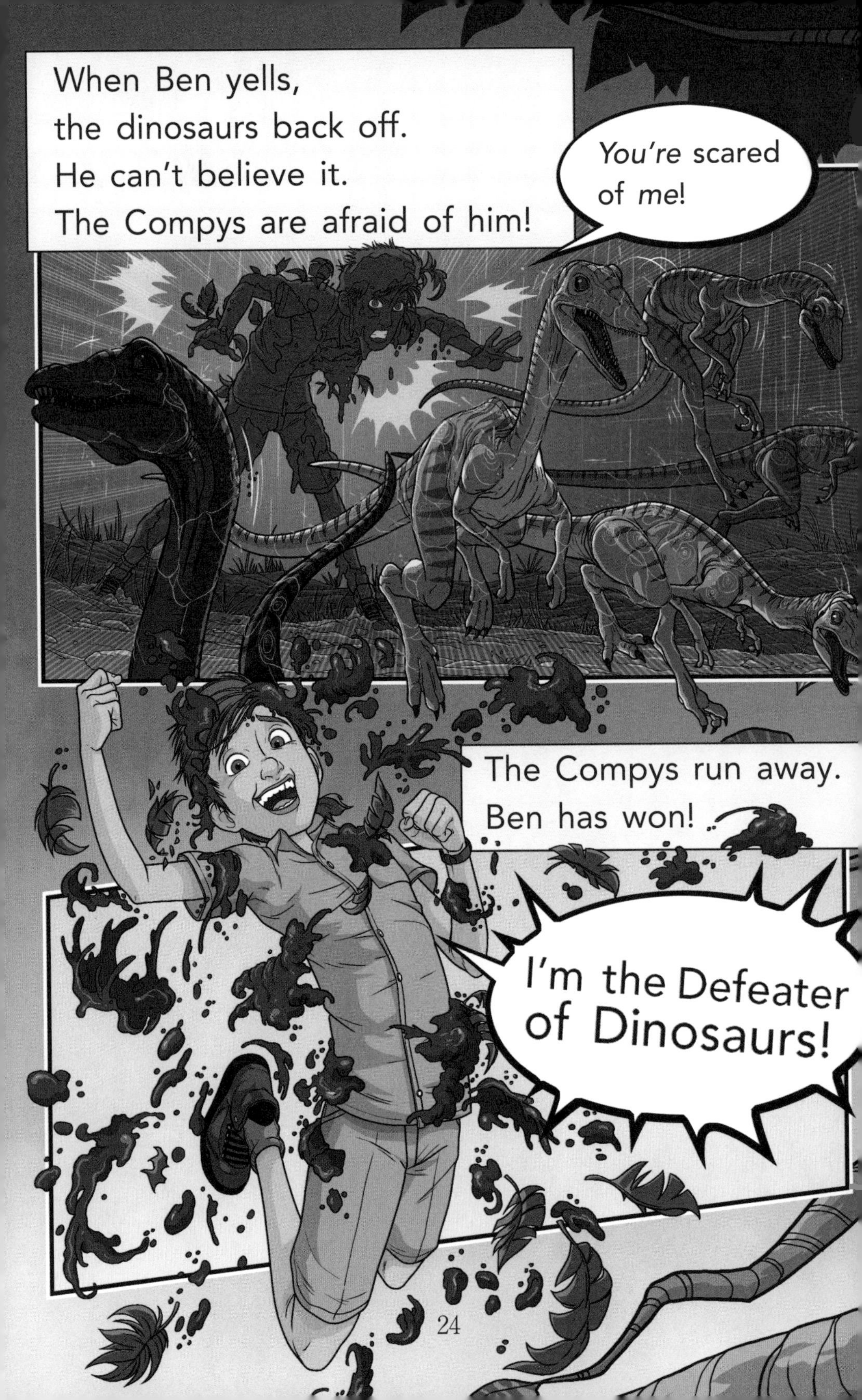
When Ben yells,
the dinosaurs back off.
He can't believe it.
The Compys are afraid of him!
You're scared of *me*!
The Compys run away.
Ben has won!
I'm the Defeater of Dinosaurs!

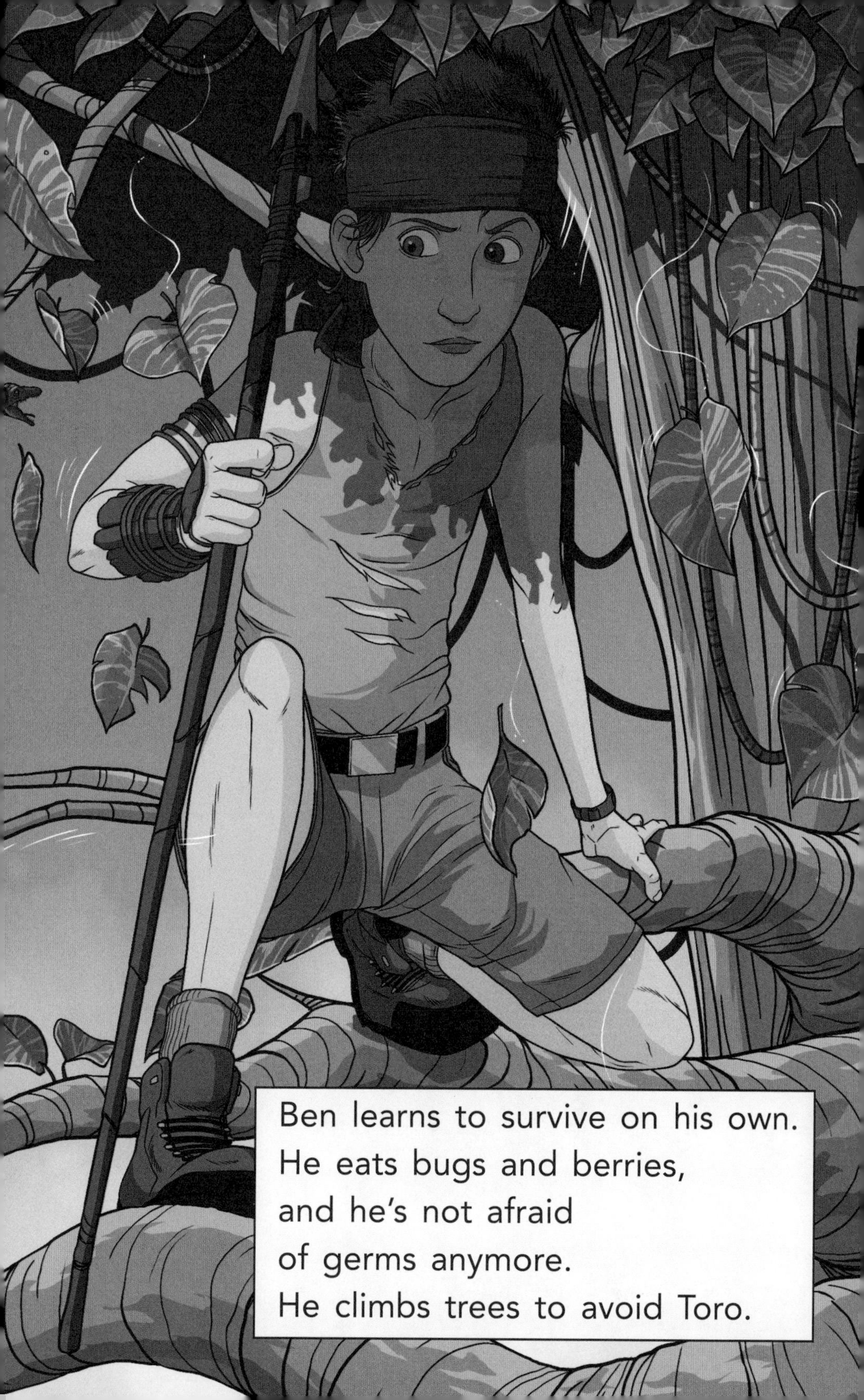

Ben learns to survive on his own.
He eats bugs and berries,
and he's not afraid
of germs anymore.
He climbs trees to avoid Toro.

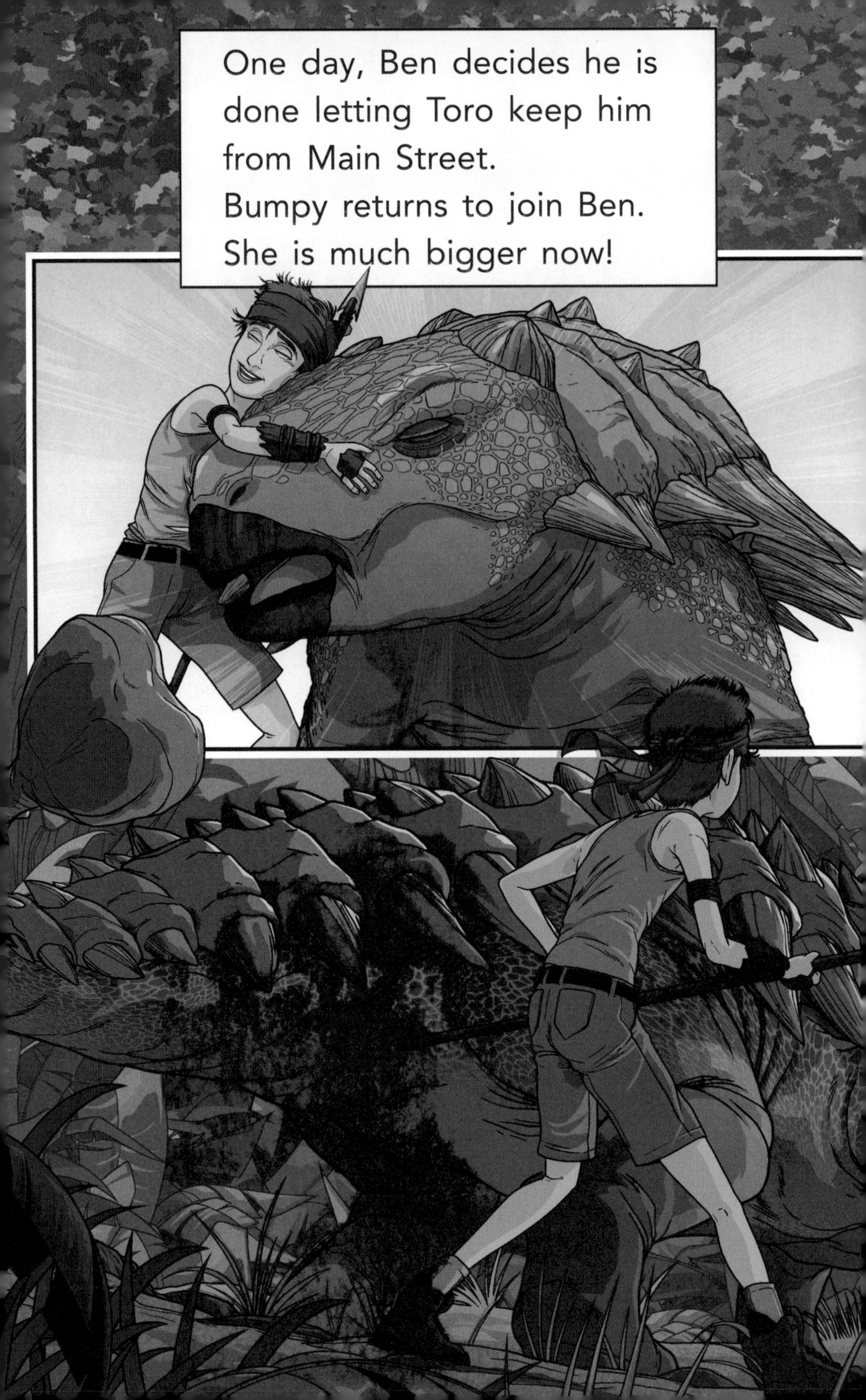
One day, Ben decides he is done letting Toro keep him from Main Street.
Bumpy returns to join Ben. She is much bigger now!

Ben is glad to have his pal back.
They face Toro together.
Ben is ready this time.
He isn't going to run away.

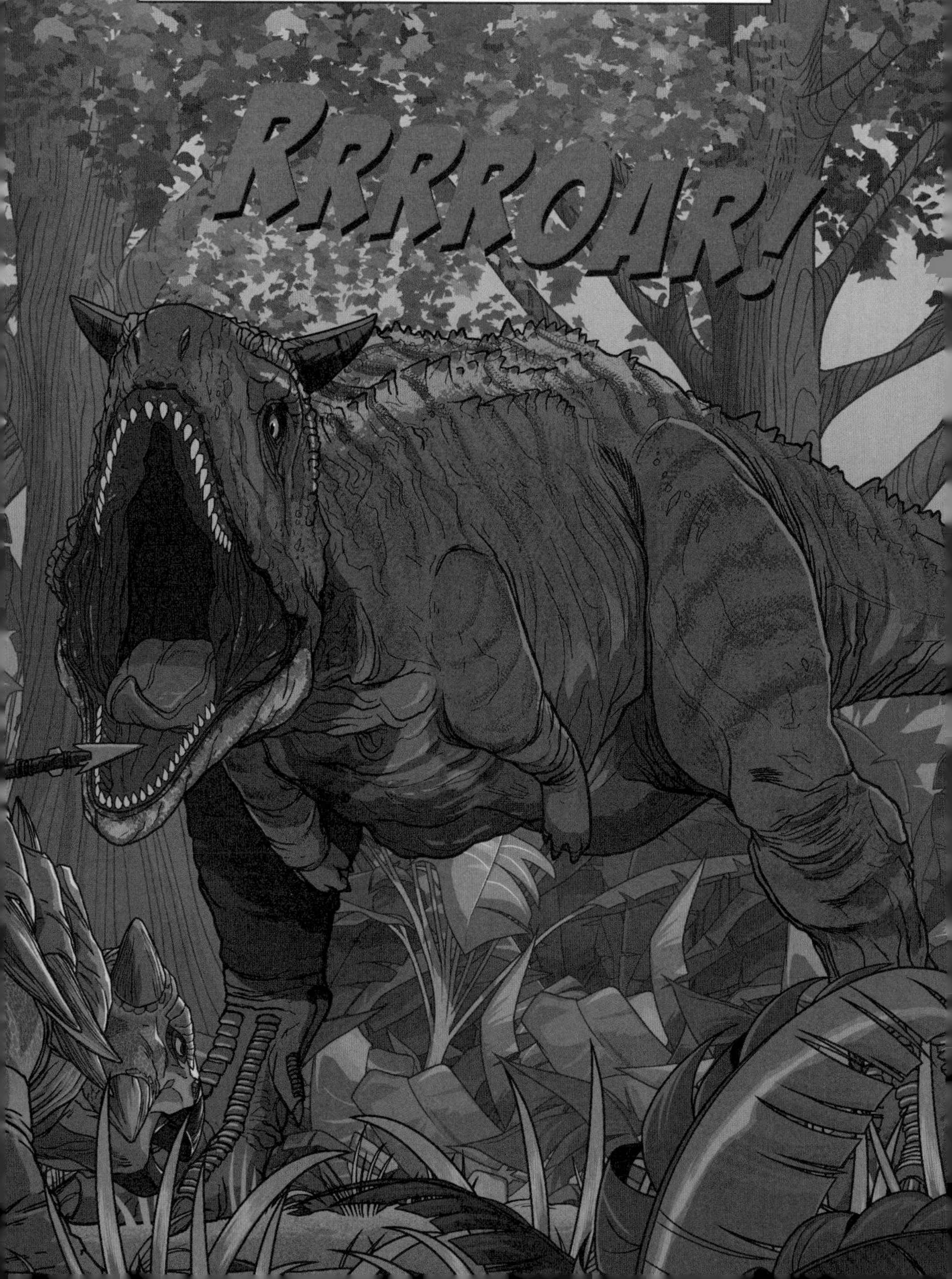
RRRROAR!

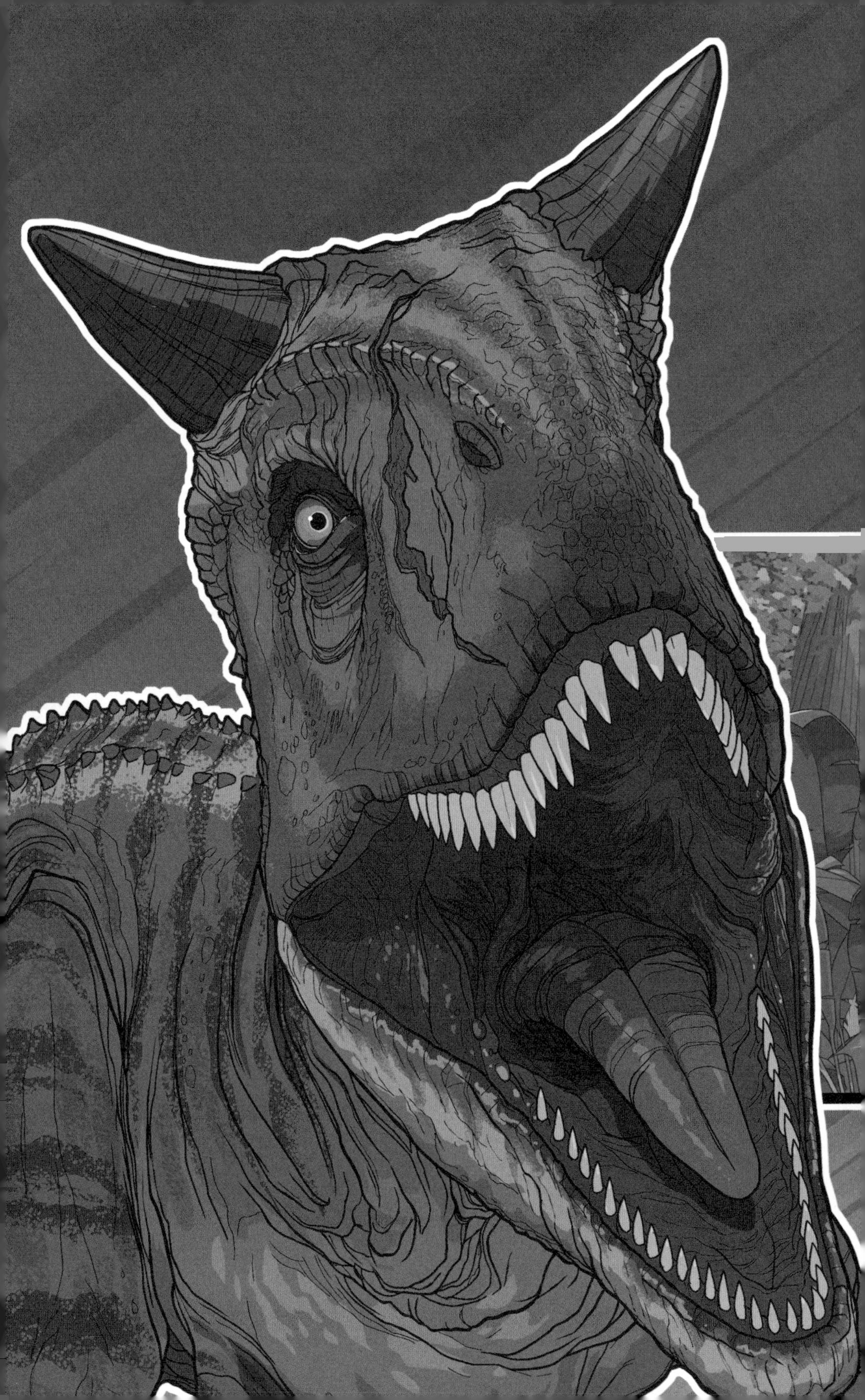

Toro runs at Ben and Bumpy.
But Ben isn't scared!
He stands his ground.

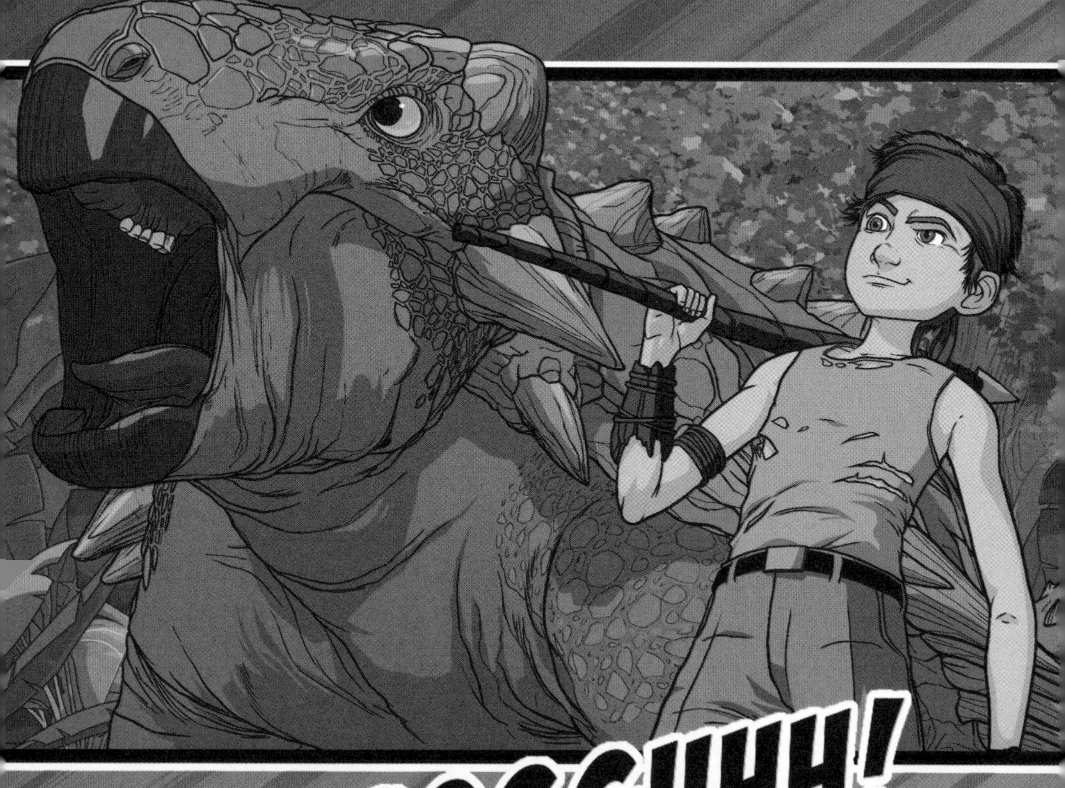
ARRRRRRGGGHHH!

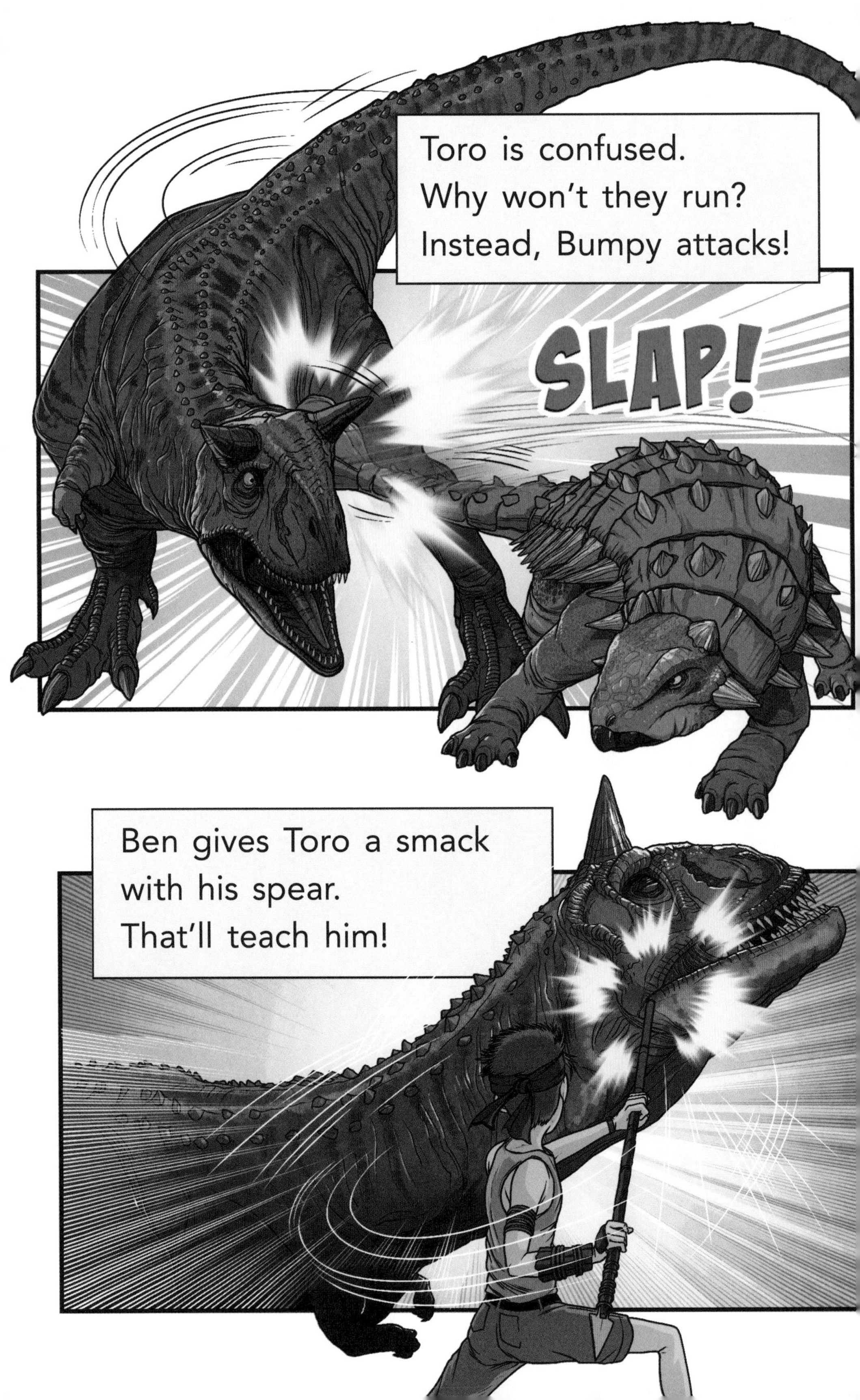
Toro is confused.
Why won't they run?
Instead, Bumpy attacks!
SLAP!
Ben gives Toro a smack
with his spear.
That'll teach him!

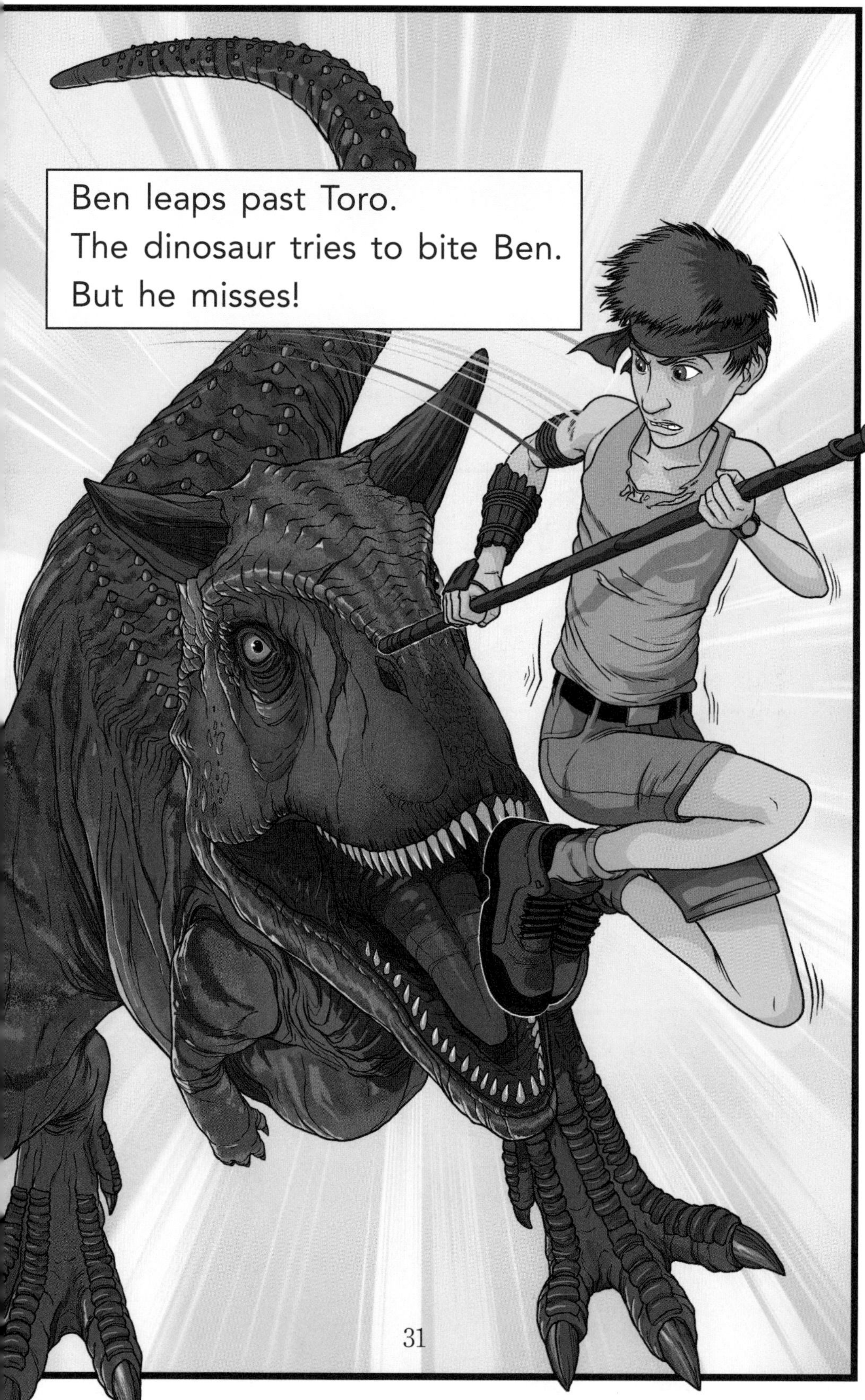
Ben leaps past Toro.
The dinosaur tries to bite Ben.
But he misses!

Ben and Bumpy escape Toro! They make it to the road . . . which means they're closer to the Main Park and to home! With his newfound courage and with Bumpy by his side, Ben is almost out of the wild!

YEEAAHHH!

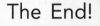

The End!